A Night in the Dinosaur Graveyard

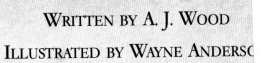

WRITTEN BY A. J. WOOD

ILLUSTRATED BY WAYNE ANDERSO

templar publishing

Professor Sponge was going on a fossil hunt.

"Can we come?" cried Lucy and Fred.

"If you must," said the Professor.
"But don't expect it to be exciting.
Fossils are not meant to be fun."

They took a bus to the edge of town.
There was a mountain valley there, deep and green.
The Professor searched for fossils by a stream.
The children played with Soap the dog.

R.I.P.
DR DIGGER
JUNE 3RD 1885

Soap began to bark. He had found a bone.
A big bone. In fact, it was the biggest bone
they had ever seen.

"This," said the Professor,
"is quite a find!"

They camped for the night in a cave in the mountainside. It was dark and cold.

Fred and Lucy were bored. The Professor snored. Then, all of a sudden, something strange happened. Something very strange indeed.

A ghostly silver shape appeared on the other side of the cave. It flickered for a minute, like a candle flame.

Then it was gone.

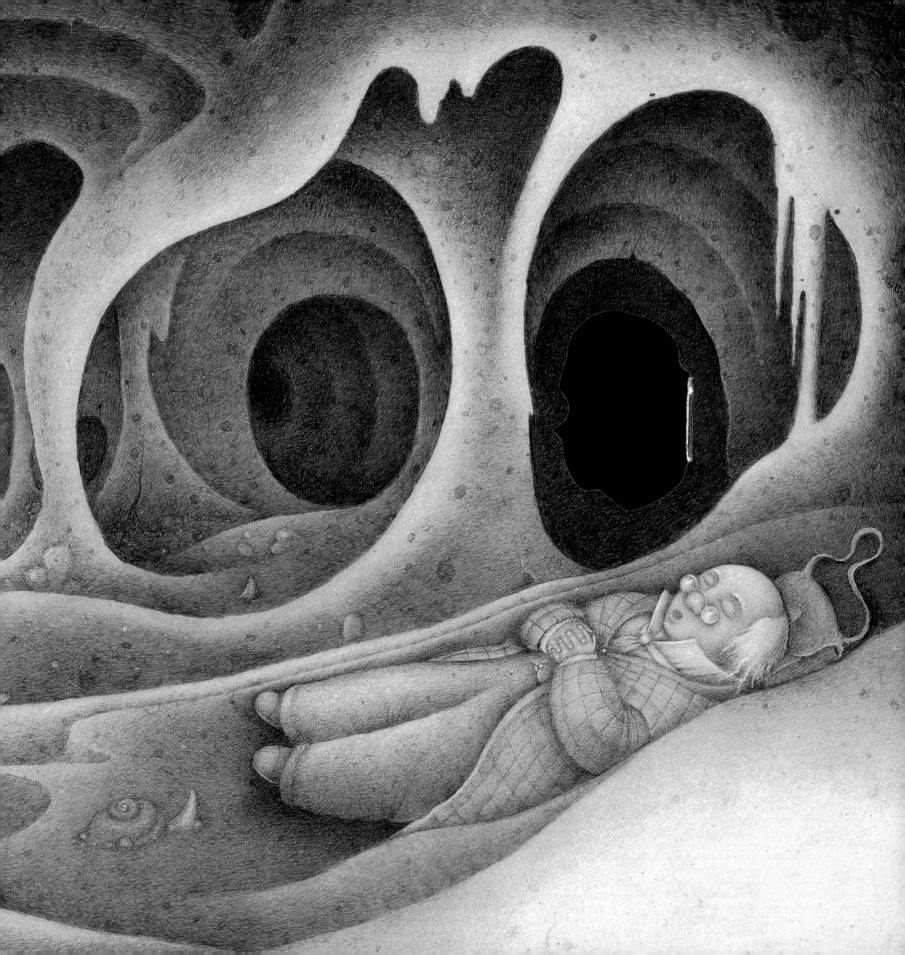

"What's going on?" said the Professor, waking up. Before they could tell him, more ghostly shapes appeared.

"They're monsters!" yelled Fred.

"They're gh-gh-ghosts!" chattered Lucy.

"They're *dinosaurs!*" said the Professor.

The dinosaur ghosts chased them round and round.

"Here's a tunnel!" shouted Fred. They dived down it, into the darkness.

"Perhaps we'll be safe here," said Lucy.
But she was wrong.

"Look out—it's a *Spinosaurus*!"
gasped the Professor.

On and on they ran, deep inside
the mountain, until...

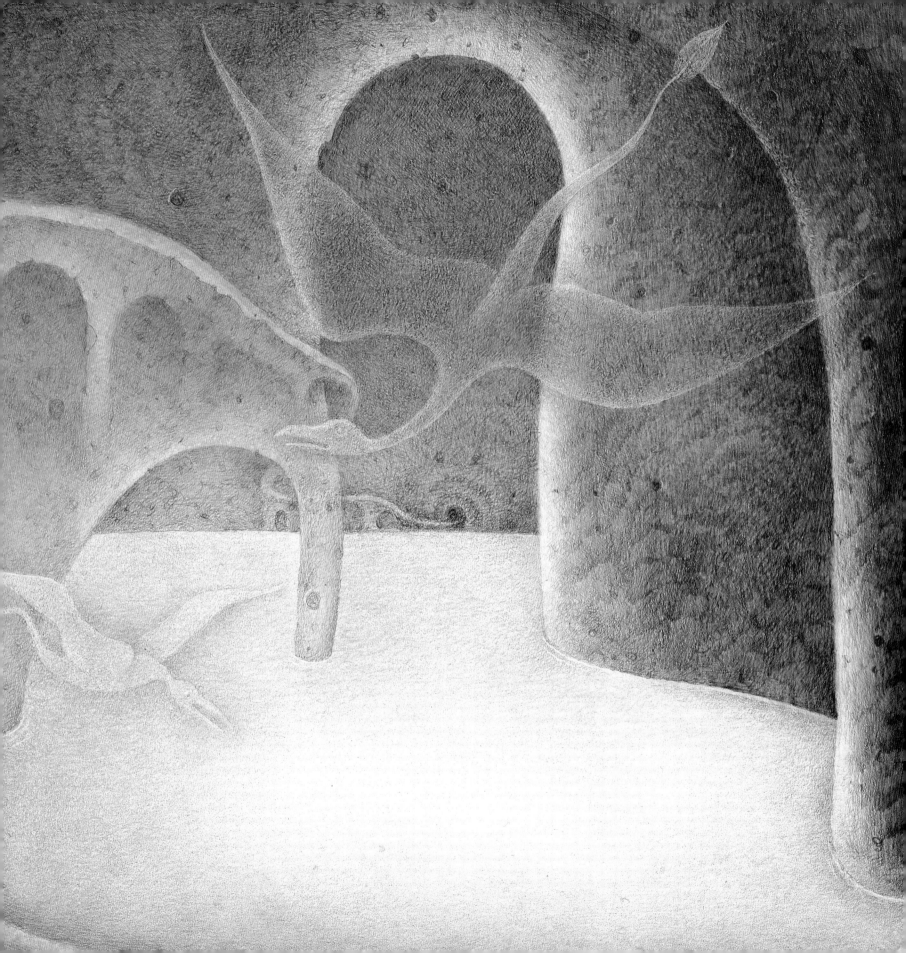

"Oh, no—a dead end!" cried Lucy.
"Unfortunate phrase," said the
Professor. "What shall we do now?"
And he leant on a boulder that,
with a huge rumble, swung silently
open like a door.

Inside there was a cavern. The dinosaurs were waiting for them.

"This is it," said the Professor. "There's no escape now!" But, just when they thought the dinosaurs were about to gobble them up, one of them stepped forward and began to speak.

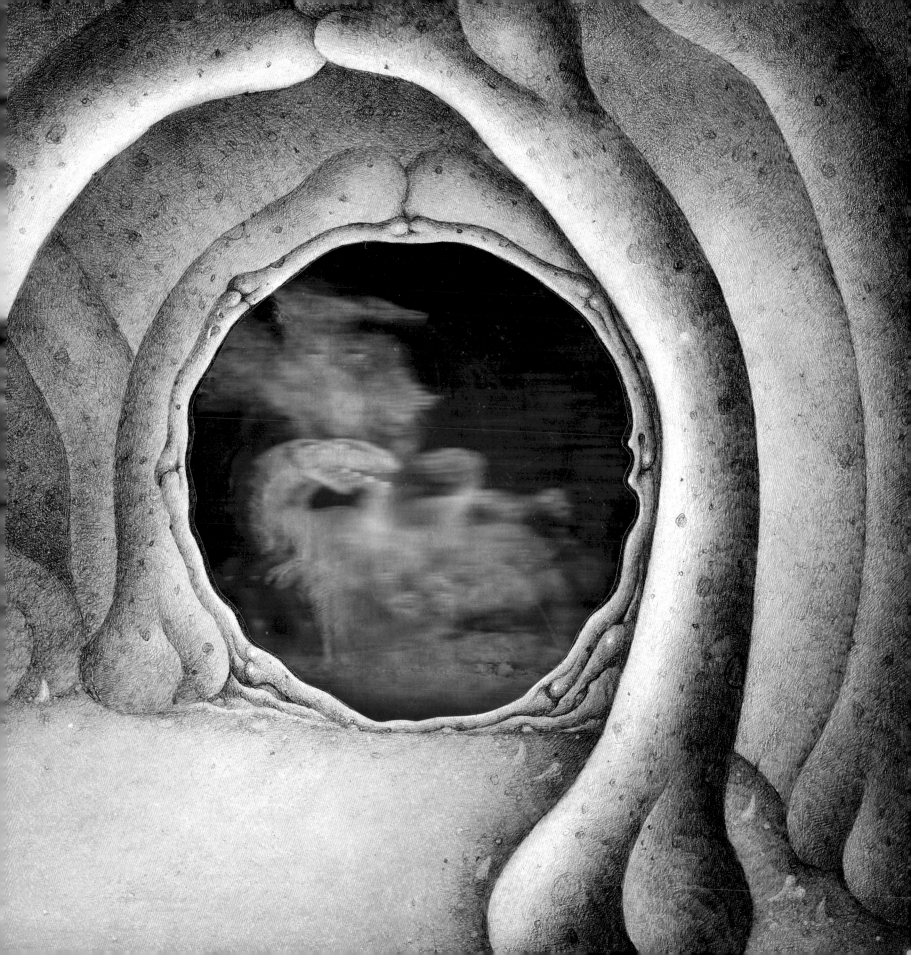

"You have entered the Dinosaur Graveyard," said the ghost. "You must give us back our bone so we may rest in peace."

"What! This bone?" said Fred, holding up the one that Soap had found.

"That's the one," said the little dinosaur. "It was stolen from us by Dr Digger, a famous fossil hunter who lived many years ago. It belongs to the dinosaur king, Tyrannosaurus Rex. You can give it back to him yourself if you wish."

"Yes please!" said the children together. They had quite forgotten to be scared.

"Follow me then," said the dinosaur. And so they did.

"Wow!" said the children.

"Woof!" said Soap, as the skeleton in front of them started to speak.

"I am Tyrannosaurus Rex, king of the dinosaurs," it said. "Thank you for bringing us back our bone. We are forever grateful." And with that, the dinosaur ghosts disappeared.